MONSTER SQUAD
RETURN OF
MEGA MANTIS

BY LAURA DOWER
ILLUSTRATED BY DAVE SCHLAFMAN
GROSSET & DUNLAP

GROSSET & DUNLAP

Published by the Penguin Group

Penguin Group (USA) Inc., 375 Hudson Street, New York, New York 10014, USA

Penguin Group (Canada), 90 Eglinton Avenue East, Suite 700, Toronto, Ontario

M4P 2Y3, Canada (a division of Pearson Penguin Canada Inc.)

Penguin Books Ltd., 80 Strand, London WC2R 0RL, England

Penguin Group Ireland, 25 St. Stephen's Green, Dublin 2, Ireland

(a division of Penguin Books Ltd.)

Penguin Group (Australia), 250 Camberwell Road, Camberwell, Victoria 3124,

Australia (a division of Pearson Australia Group Pty. Ltd.)

Penguin Books India Pvt. Ltd., 11 Community Centre,

Panchsheel Park, New Delhi–110 017, India

Penguin Group (NZ), 67 Apollo Drive, Rosedale, North Shore 0632, New Zealand

(a division of Pearson New Zealand Ltd.)

Penguin Books (South Africa) (Pty.) Ltd., 24 Sturdee Avenue,

Rosebank, Johannesburg 2196, South Africa

Penguin Books Ltd., Registered Offices: 80 Strand, London WC2R 0RL, England

Library of Congress Control Number: 2009001250

ISBN 978-0-448-44913-5   10 9 8 7 6 5 4 3 2 1

For Papa.

—Laura Dower

To the hardest worker I know . . .
I love you, Mom.

—Dave Schlafman

TABLE OF CONTENTS

PROLOGUE

DAMON
MOLLOY

I sleep like a rock. But this morning, I heard a noise so loud and so strange that I thought my house kerploded. My eyes popped open.

The first thing I saw was my six-foot poster of Chomp-O the Magnificent.

"Aaaaah!" I cried and slipped off the bed. I landed hard on the floor. Good thing it was covered with dirty laundry and tube socks.

I glared at Chomp-O.

"Thanks for scaring me, bud," I said, pulling myself back onto the bed.

For the past few days I've heard noises like weird squeals and clanks coming from far away. But this noise seemed closer, like it was right in our backyard.

Mom and Dad think I need to get my ears checked.

They don't hear anything. And my sister Rachel says she hears the same stuff I do, but she's not a reliable witness. Rachel claims there are imaginary voices coming from her stuffed dolls and bears.

My Chomp-O Souvenir Digital Clock read 5:23 AM, as in *almost morning*. It was way too early to start the day for real.

I scrunched down under Cowboy Pete. That's my favorite comforter. I've had it since I was three, and it has holes everywhere, but Pete makes me feel safe.

I wanted to fall asleep again, but my mind was racing. I expected to hear the weird noise again. But all I heard was the gurgle of my fish tank.

There was no going back to sleep now. I clicked off the alarm clock.

There's a very good reason why I am so freaked out by all these strange noises. It all comes down to one thing: B-Monsters.

B-Monsters are the fake-looking monsters with weird names that step on cities with their enormous claws and breathe laughing gas all over.

Lately, I have those monsters on the brain— big time.

Reason #1: I live in Riddle, otherwise known

as home to the Bs. Oswald Leery lives here, too, smack-dab in the middle of Riddle. He's the famous director who invented B-Monster Vision, a special 3-D filming process. He lives in his own creepy castle, way up on top of Nerve Mountain.

Reason #2: My parents own the Drive-O-Rama out on Route 5. That's where all of Leery's original B-Monster movies were screened for the first time. My grandparents were actually *friends* with Leery. Mom brags that she delivered me inside the Drive-O-Rama's Snack Shack during a midnight showing of Oswald Leery's classic, *Martian Mayhem*.

Reason #3: Three weeks ago, I learned the most incredible secret ever.

B-Monsters are really and truly *real*.

It all started at a special library screening of *Slimo*. I only went because Ms. Shenanigans, our librarian, said we'd meet the real Oswald Leery up close. What a scam! Instead of Leery, we got his assistant, Walter. Later, we found out that Leery never even intended to come to the screening. He just wanted to set up a few fifth-graders from Riddle Elementary—including me, Jesse Ranger, Stella Min, and Lindsey Gomez. So he had Walter recruit us for this B-Monster-butt-kicking group called Monster Squad. Walter told us Leery's B-Monsters were coming to life each time an original movie reel was shown. He needed us to kill the B-Monsters, destroy the movie reels, and, while we were at it, save the world.

No sweat, right?

I would never have believed this were possible if I hadn't seen a real B-Monster with my own eyes. Right after we formed the squad, we met a green, gooey one: Slimo! At one point, I was up to my eyebrows in green monster snot, and let me tell you, Slimo does *not* smell too good.

But together, the Monster Squad got the goo and saved our science teacher, Mr. Bunsen, at the same time. Then we shredded the original *Slimo* reel. Too cool!

Somehow, our differences made us work well as a group. Jesse Ranger is the brains. He's so smart he can read a book and write a book report at the same time. Stella Min's our squad muscle. Everyone at school calls her Ninja because she's not afraid to take on anything; not even a slimy B-Monster. Lindsey Gomez is the squad clown. Her jokes are bad, but we all laugh. I think Lindsey is here for comic relief.

And then there's me. I'm the B-Monster almanac. Name a movie and I can name the theme song, supporting cast, and license plate number on the getaway car.

"Damon! Get it in gear, son! School!"

Dad was calling from downstairs. The Chomp-O clock read 7:42 already. Time sure flies when I'm thinking about the Bs.

There were now only twenty-three minutes left to dress, eat, brush, and motor over to the Riddle Elementary School bus stop with my warthog of a little sister, Rachel.

I quickly got up, yanked a T-shirt over my head, and laced up my black high-tops. Walking to the door, I heard something. It stopped me cold.

Sqweeeeeeeeeeeeeeeeeeeeeeee.

I dashed to the window to check it out.

But there was nothing in the side yard. I couldn't see the front yard. Was there something in the field *behind* our house? I needed time to explore.

But there was no time.

"DAMON!"

"Aaaaaaah!"

The bedroom door flung open and my little

rat of a sister just stood there in her pink fleece, smirking.

"Rachel!" I grabbed for the doorknob. "The door will stick!"

"You're in big trouble!" Rachel whined with that na-na-na voice she always gets. "Dad's extra-grouchy and now you're late and you better get ready—"

"And you better *get out*!" I yelled. I bent down, picked up a shoe, and threw it at her. Unfortunately, I missed.

Rachel stuck out her tongue. "I'm telling!" Then she made this throw-up face and pointed at my head. "Eeeeeew! There are bugs on your head!"

"Bugs?"

Just hearing the word made my pulse race.

I spun around to the mirror and held my breath.

Sure enough, two big, fat flies were sitting on my head!

Bzzzzzzzzzt! Bzzzzzzt!

A regular kid would have shaken those flies onto the floor and stomped until they were a puddle of bug. But I didn't. I couldn't. I am not *regular* when it comes to bugs.

"Get them off!" I waved my arms in the air. "OFF!"

The startled flies buzzed up to the ceiling.

That was when I saw the *other* flies. There must have been twenty huddled together on the outside windowpane.

"Look at the flies!" I cried. "We have to get Dad!"

"Race ya!" Rachel cried, running for my door. She darted ahead of me and pulled the door shut.

"Nooooooo!"

It was too late. The door was stuck closed. I was trapped with the bugs.

"Go get Dad," I cried.

Bzzzzzzzzzt! Bzzzzzzt!

I looked at the ceiling and then at the window. There were now at least *fifty* more flies on the window in addition to the fat two inside my room. I felt woozy. The bugs appeared out of nowhere. It was just like the time Slimo appeared in my bathroom out of nowhere . . .

Gulp.

Did that mean we were about to get another B-Monster—with wings this time?

Nervously, I backed away from the window and huddled in the corner of the bedroom, far away from the flies.

"Daaaaaad!" I wailed as loudly as I could. "Help! Bug!"

All at once, my bedroom door flew open again. Dad rushed in waving a super-sized fly swatter.

"Let me at 'em!" Dad cried, swatting like a swashbuckler. Unlike me, Dad isn't scared of

anything. I guess you get superhero nerves of steel when you screen scary Bs for a living.

Dad spotted the flies on the ceiling right away. Without missing a beat, he raised the swatter and—

THWACK!

One swat. Two flies. *Now that's skill.*

They dropped dead onto my bed.

"Come on, Damon." Dad sighed as he picked up the flattened bugs between his fingertips. "Time for school."

CHAPTER 1

TEAM SHMEEM

"Just serve the ball already!" someone called out to me from across the gym. I flashed a smile at Pat and Seamus, my two best buddies in class. Then I turned around and pretended to pull down my gym shorts.

"Hey, Mr. Molloy!" Coach Dunne barked. He blew his whistle hard. "I'm watching you. No funny stuff!"

I tossed the volleyball over my head and jumped up to slam my serve.

Swooosh!

My volleyball soared up and over the net, dropping straight to the floor right between two kids.

"Now that's what I'm talking about!" I shouted. I went to high-five Pat, but then, at the last minute, I pulled my hand away.

"Ha!" I cried. He always fell for that one.

Pat grabbed my shirt hard like he wanted to wrestle me.

"Hey! Don't touch the merchandise," I said, brushing off my T-shirt. The front of today's shirt read *Jokeman*.

I moved from serving position to the front of the court. On the opposite side, facing me, was Tate the Great, the biggest kid in our entire class. Tate eats three sandwiches and drinks five milks every day for lunch. But whenever we're in gym class, I eat *him* for lunch on the court. I saw him staring at me. I stared right back, like a sumo.

"Mr. Molloy!" Coach called over. "I'd like you to step out of the game for a while, please. Tap Miss Min on your way in."

I held up my hands. "Huh? What did I do?" I said. Out of the corner of my eye, I saw Tate the Great. He grinned and waved at me.

"Buh-bye, Jokeman," Tate said.

"I'll be back," I muttered under my breath. Then I headed for Stella. "Yo, Ninja," I said and reached out to tap her shoulder. "Coach says it's your turn."

Stella growled at me. "Don't even think about touching me, Molloy. I bite."

"Yeah," I growled back. "And you smell, too." Then I tapped her on the shoulder anyway. She couldn't do anything about it because Coach was watching.

From my seat on the sidelines, I watched Jesse Ranger and his friend Garth Gable goof around at the net. Those two try, but they couldn't volley their way out of a duffel bag. They definitely couldn't get Tate to go down.

A serve zipped over the net like a bullet. Someone from the other side whacked it back. It was headed for Garth!

Oh, great, I thought. I buried my face in my hands. This would be too painful to watch. But the incredible happened. Garth set up the ball—*perfectly*. Ranger came down on it like a hammer. It spiked over the net, right into Tate's face!

He didn't see that coming.

"Now that's what I'm talking about!"

Everyone cheered, including me. Ever since this Monster Squad thing started, I've been trying to be more of a team player. It doesn't come easy. But that cheer just flew right out of me.

"Hey, Damon," Ranger said, running over. "Don't forget the squad meeting right after school."

"Right," I said. He rushed away before I had a chance to tell him about the flies and the noises in my bedroom that morning. I'd save it for the meeting.

On the way to the playground that afternoon, Pat and Seamus saw me. Ever since this whole Monster Squad thing started, it's been a little awkward with them.

"Yo!" I called out, waving. "What's up?"

"What's up with *you*, Damon?" Seamus cried. "We were looking for you! Can Pat and I come over and play Laser Bikes? You got it, right?"

"Yes!" I cried. My parents just bought me a Z-Pack with all these games, including Laser Bikes. Pat and Seamus hadn't seen it yet.

"Come over!" I said. Then I caught myself. "Oh, wait. I can't do it today. I have this . . . *thing*."

"Thing?" Pat said, mocking me.

"Then text us later," Seamus said with a shrug.

"Later," I grumbled. Once again I had to choose between Monster Squad and my buddies. Pat and Seamus walked away without me.

I swung my body up and over the monkey bars. When I hang by my knees and all the blood rushes to my head, I can think better. I hung there for a few minutes, watching the kids come out of school. Ranger, Stella, and Lindsey were nowhere to be seen.

Had I gotten the meeting place wrong?

BUZZZZZZZZZZZZZZT.

What was that?

I flipped off the bar and landed on all fours.

BUZZZZZZZZZZZZZZT.

Not ten feet from me was a swarm of black and yellow bees.

"Beeeeeeeees!"

I waved my arms all over the place and wailed. A couple of kids on the swings gave me dirty looks. Couldn't they see the insect attack that was taking place?

Without the rest of the Monster Squad to back me up, all I could do was run.

I thought I could shake the bees with some fast

footwork, but they shadowed me all the way home. Before I knew it, I was standing under the Cicada Lane sign at my corner.

It figures that I live on a street named after a bug.

For some reason, my neighborhood was a ghost town. Crusty old Mr. Wombat wasn't mowing his lawn. The Parker twins weren't on their swing set. Even Wacko, the neighborhood dog, was missing in action.

But the bees were still here!

BUZZZZZZZZZZZZZZT.

I raced up our driveway. Where was Mom's car? I thought hard. She probably took Rachel to ballet class. And Dad was probably at the Drive-O-Rama, working as usual.

BUZZZZZZZZZZZZZZT.

I dug into my jeans' pocket for my house key. The bugs began to buzz around my face and neck. It seemed like there were more of them by the second!

Finally, the key slid into the lock.

But it wouldn't twist!

"GO AWAY, I DON'T LIKE YOU!" I yelled at the

bees. I was nearly hysterical. Then I heard another noise!

Sqweeeeeeeeeeeeeeeeeeeeeeeeeeeeeeee.

Come on key, I thought. *Open! OPEN!*

Sqweeeeeeeeeeeeeeeeeeeeeeeeeeeeeeee.

Frantically, I pushed the house door open and threw my book bag onto our hall bench. The door slammed behind me. The bees were locked out—at least for now.

SQUEEEEEEEEEEEEEE.

I sprinted upstairs to my bedroom window for a better view. My eyes scanned the field.

Nothing to the right . . .

Nothing down the middle . . .

There!

I gasped at a broad shadow stretched across the left side of the field.

What *was* that?

The shadow was way too big for anything normal in my backyard. It was so tall it seemed to touch the sky. There were long black things sticking up into the air. There was a loud, awful crunch . . .

Hold on! Was that *chewing*? Were those *antennae*?

Suddenly the black thing moved closer and I could see exactly what it was.

Oh no!

Out there in my backyard was a living, breathing, giant BUG!

CHAPTER 2

AN ARMADA OF MINIATURE UFOs

"Heeeeelp!" I wailed and ran downstairs, all the way to the basement. On the way down, I grabbed our portable phone.

I called Ranger first, but the phone just rang. Of course he wasn't home. The Monster Squad was at the playground for our meeting!

That meant there was a giant bug in my backyard and no one to help me.

"Get a grip, Damon," I told myself. Was a real, live B-Monster in my yard? There was no other logical explanation.

"Damon!"

Mom?

My mother and sister were back home! I grabbed the phone and darted down the stairs to the living room. I had never been so excited to see them in my entire life, but I couldn't let them see me this scared.

"Damon?" Mom gazed right into my pupils when she saw me. "Is everything okay, dear? Do you have a fever? You look pale."

"Ha!" Rachel snorted. "You look *freaked out*."

"No," I groaned. "Just tired."

"Well," Mom said, tousling my hair. "Don't you have studying to do? Isn't your math test this week?"

"Yes," I sighed. "Thanks for reminding me."

Just talking about tests made my mouth go dry. Math tests are almost as scary as giant B-Monsters. *Almost.*

"Well, get to it," Mom said, giving me a goofy thumbs-up. She and Rachel walked out.

The moment they left, I ran to the window and scanned the back field. Soon the sky would darken and it would be harder to see. Was the shadow bug still out there? Or had my eyes been playing tricks on me?

I wanted so badly to tell Mom and Rachel the truth about the shadow bug and the gnats and all about Oswald Leery, too. But the squad made a promise to keep real B-Monsters a big secret.

And I don't break promises.

I worked on my math for a little while, but I was having trouble concentrating. I couldn't believe that Mom wanted me to study right now. How was I supposed to do math homework with that *thing* in our yard?

I went over to the window to check for the big bug again. It had gotten dark, but I could see something coming toward me. It was a row of itty, bitty lights illuminating everything below it. The lights looked just like these teeny spaceships I'd read about in one of Dr. Leery's *B-Monster Galaxy* magazines.

But once the lights came closer, I realized I wasn't watching spaceships. These were bugs. Lightning bugs! There must have been a thousand! They swooped in like an armada of miniature UFOs, but they were definitely bugs.

"Moooooom!" I screamed.

"Damon?" Mom asked, rushing back into the living room. "What is the matter?"

I pointed out the window. The bugs were multiplying by the second, just like the flies and bees. Their light was so bright it lit up the whole backyard.

"Damon, are you feeling all right?" Mom asked. She gently put her arm around my shoulders. "Sit down."

"But the bugs!" I pointed to the window. "The whole sky is lit up right there. Can't you see?"

"Are you playing a joke on me?" Mom laughed. "I'm not falling for it, Damon!"
Why didn't Mom see them?

"Come on," Mom continued. "Let's cook dinner. How about burgers?"

"With flies? I mean *fries*?" I sighed.

"Flies?" Mom laughed. She patted my head like a puppy. "I think you've been working too hard, dear. You have bugs on the brain."

I wished Mom could see what I saw. But of course she couldn't see the bugs, just like she couldn't see Slimo when I found goo coming out of my bathroom sink. Only the Monster Squad, Leery, Walter, and a few others had the power to see when a monster was a real, live B.

But which B was out there right now?

Island of Dr. Dim?

Asteroidia, Terror from Deep Space?

Beware of the Bees?

I remembered movie titles, but I couldn't get my details straight. My mind was spinning. Did the B bee movie have flies? Did the fly movie have bees? If only I had made it to the Monster Squad meeting today. My fellow squad members probably could have helped me figure out which B was which.

"Damon! Let's go!" Mom called from the kitchen.

"Just a sec!" I called back. Then I grabbed the phone. I speed-dialed Ranger again.

Hopefully he would be home by now.

CHAPTER 3

ANOTHER
BADVENTURE

This time Ranger picked up the phone. I told him everything.

After that, I called the girls. The four of us agreed to do a few things as soon as humanly possible:

1. ID the B (for sure).

2. Get to Leery Castle and tell Walter and Leery *everything*.

3. Whomp that B-Monster and save the world.

The next morning, I was revved to go. Rachel stayed home sick so I went to school alone. Excellent! But just as I stepped onto our front porch, I heard something go *smoosh* under my sneaker. I lifted my shoe. It looked like gum. Green gum.

But it wasn't gum. These were green bugs: tiny

praying mantids hopping all over the place. Some were dead, but most had their tiny legs folded up like they were praying for real. I could feel their little black eyes on me.

"WHY ME?" I screamed. I would have given anything for a bottle of Bug-Off right about now.

I leaped over a cluster and ran toward the street.

But even after I'd made it off the porch, I was not bug-free. Something else tickled my cheek and I swatted.

No way! Now a mini swarm of gnats chased me! And the harder I tried to shoo them away, the closer they hovered.

"Get off!" I wailed, slapping my neck and arms and neck again. I dashed for the school bus stop, bobbing and weaving like a prizefighter.

But nothing shook off these gnats!

When the kids at the bus stop saw me coming, one yelled, "What's your problem?"

Everyone was staring. A few kids doubled over with laughter at the sight of me. One pack of kids shuffled away from me as if I had cooties.

And the truth was I *did* have them. I had gnatties!

Play it cool, I told myself. But when the swarm swooped in at me again, I flapped my arms like a chicken. These gnats were flying so close to my face that I could barely blink without a bug getting caught in my lashes!

I usually love being the center of attention, but this was too much.

Where's an Invisibility Cloak when you really need one?

"Damon?"

I turned around, swatting.

"Ranger!"

Ranger made a face. "Gee, you weren't kidding when you said you saw weird bugs everywhere. You're covered in fleas."

"Gnats!"

"Same difference," Ranger said.

I raised my eyebrow. "You should have seen the praying mantids on my porch!"

"Mantids? Praying? About what?"

"There were hundreds. They looked like . . ."

I stopped mid-sentence. It dawned on me that I knew *exactly* what those mantids looked like. Of course! They were miniature versions of the giant bug shadow I saw in my backyard . . .

"Mega Mantis!" I yelled out. "The new B-Monster in town is Mega Mantis! That's it!"

"Huh?" Ranger said with disbelief. "Are you serious?"

Scenes from the original B-Monster *Mega Mantis* flick popped into my head. "Yes! Of course! Remember the pond scene?" I asked Ranger.

"Yes! When the bugs swarmed out of nowhere?"

"And attacked that little dog and carried him up into the sky?"

"Mega turned that pooch into a chew toy!" Ranger cried.

I shuddered. "I got swarm nightmares for weeks."

Ranger waved his hands around my head. Now *I* was the swarm nightmare.

"But remember what Roger Rogers says in the movie?" Ranger asked.

Rogers was one of the big heroes in Oswald Leery's Bs. We all wanted to be as brave as Roger Rogers.

"Of course I remember!" I said.

Together, we recited his most famous line from the movie. "Don't mess with me. And don't mess with the mantis!"

Then, from down the street, the school bus pulled into view.

"Aha!" I cried.

I put on my best ugly face and we muscled our way to the front of the bus line. We thought for sure that the gnats would follow. But strangely, the bugs headed for the bus headlights instead.

What a lucky break. They like lights even more than me!

The driver opened the doors and Ranger and I scrambled onto the bus. We collapsed in a backseat. I thought the gnats were gone for good. Then, a half mile down the road, my gigantic gnat swarm came back! The swarm showed up just outside my bus window. It looked like the swarm of flies from my bedroom window the day before.

Some people have animal magnetism; I guess I must have bug magnetism.

"Pssst!" Ranger whispered. "Remember in *Mega Mantis*, how all the people get followed by swarms? But the insects don't swarm onto the bus to City Hall?"

"Right!" I said. "They won't enter a moving vehicle!"

"We should contact Oswald Leery," Ranger said. "I think we're in big bug trouble."

"Yeah," I mumbled. "We need an emergency Monster Squad meeting. Sorry I missed the last one . . ."

"That's okay. You're still in the squad," Ranger said.

I punched him in the shoulder with a smile. "Better be," I said.

I complained a lot about my fellow Monster Squad members, but the truth was they weren't all *that* dorky. Lindsey was nice. Stella was tough. Ranger was smart. We really were in this together.

Now if I could just figure out how to move from the school bus into the school building without getting swarmed, I'd be all set.

CHAPTER 4

YOU'RE GNATS!

When the bus rounded the cul-de-sac outside the school's main doors, Ranger and I planned our mad dash inside. If we moved fast enough, we could beat the gnats.

We covered our heads with our jackets and sprinted for the doors.

It worked!

When the bugs didn't follow us inside, I thought maybe they'd leave us alone for a while. But the very first period, in the middle of my math test, I spotted something suspicious outside the classroom window.

The swarm! There must have been a thousand gnats! There were so many I think they began to block out the sun. I wanted to jump up and shout, "Excuse me, but doesn't anyone else see what's going on?"

But then I remembered: Only a few of us could see them.

As soon as the class bell rang, Monster Squad gathered in the hall. We kept our voices low.

"Did you see that?" Lindsey whispered.

I nodded. "A swarm like the one we saw outside the school bus window."

I told everyone again about the bugs in my yard and the giant shadow I'd seen the night before. I was *certain* the bugs meant a genuine B-Monster was lurking around and that that B-Monster was Mega Mantis.

"We need to keep track of all these details," Stella said, as serious as ever.

"I'll take plenty of pictures for reference," Lindsey said, holding up her Sure Shot digital camera.

One of our fifth-grade teachers actually nicknamed Lindsey "Paparazzi," just because she brings her camera everywhere. I think she always wears it because she wants to be like her grandpa Max. Max took pictures for B-Monster Studios back in the day.

As Lindsey snapped, my palms got sweatier. All these bugs were making me so nervous. If they kept following me, I wasn't sure I'd be able to stay on this Monster Squad mission. Meeting Mega face-to-face would give me hives.

"We need to do something!" Stella said. "This is one serious situation."

I groaned. Stella walks around Riddle like she just drank a big cup of serious. And she acts tough like a ninja *all the time*, whether she's in the karate studio or out.

I tried hard to think of something clever to say. I was about to speak, when something nipped at me. I reached for my neck.

"Yowch!" I cried. "One of the gnats bit me!" *How had it gotten inside?*

Ranger held his hands up. "Oh no! Bugs are making contact. We don't have much time. I think we should head up to Leery Castle after school. Walter will help us."

We all nodded. On the Stella serious scale, this was definitely a ten-plus.

I watched the clock all day. When the end-of-day school bell rang, my nerve was back. The bugs had disappeared after lunch. I hadn't seen a swarm—or even a lone gnat—in three whole hours. The moment the bell rang at the end of school, I met up with the others. We raced to the public bus stop, ready for the second official Monster Squad mission.

Lindsey couldn't resist pulling out her camera.

"Say mozzarella!" Lindsey said, snapping. I made a funny face. Why can't that girl just say, "Say cheese!" like a normal person?

"Hey, Lindsey!" Stella yelled. "Take a photo of *that*!"

"Incoming!" Ranger cried. "What a cloud!"

"That's too dark to be a cloud," I cried, looking up. "Those are the gnats from outside the classroom!"

It looked like the swarm we'd been watching all day, only much, *much* wider.

"What's the matter, Damon? *Scared* of a few bugs?" Stella teased.

"No! I don't get scared, remember?" I snapped, trying to sound *tuff* like the word across the front of my T-shirt.

Stella laughed. "Yeah, sure you don't get scared." She assumed her most menacing karate stance. "I know how to handle a pack like that! Kiiiiya!"

I rolled my eyes. "First of all, the bugs are still miles away, Ninja. And second of all, you can't karate-chop a pack of gnats, even if the cloud comes closer! I think that's physically impossible."

"Who says I can't do it?" Stella snapped at me. "I can do whatever I want!"

Lindsey stepped in between us. "Guys, you can't fight each other and expect to fight a B-Monster, too."

"I think the cloud really is getting closer!" Ranger shouted.

Thankfully, no other people waiting for the bus could see the cloud like we could. They didn't know it was made of bugs. They still believed the darkness was just a storm front. Maybe they thought we were doing some kind of rain dance.

Thankfully, we piled onto the bus before the cloud came any closer.

The ride seemed normal at first, except for the fact that my heart was beating like a bongo. Then, as we passed Round Ridge, the bus lurched. A warning bell went off. The driver turned off the engine.

Oh no, I thought to myself. *We can't stop. Not now.*

"Attention, passengers," the driver said. "We need to pull over for just a few moments. There's a funny clunk in the trunk so I called dispatch for a service truck. I don't want any of you to get stuck up on the mountain. From the looks of the sky out there, there's bad weather coming, too, so I need to be extra careful . . ."

The other passengers began whispering and moving around. Ranger nudged me.

"A clunk in the trunk? What do you think is *really* going on?" he whispered.

"Maybe Mega Mantis is up ahead," I said.

Stella glared. "SHHHHHH!"

"It can't really be Mega," she whispered.

"Maybe the bus is really broken," Ranger replied.

A passenger standing next to us frowned. He peered out at the sky. "I didn't know it was supposed to rain today," he said.

"It's not!" I cried. "But we think that might be a—"

"SHHHHH!" Stella slapped her hand over my mouth.

The man gave us a funny look and moved to the other side of the bus.

"Are *you* insane?" Stella hissed. "You can't tell

strangers about what's *really* going on. You'll cause a panic!"

"Actually, Stella," Ranger said, "panic may be our best option. That cloud is really close to the bus now. I think we need to do something."

"Like what?" Stella cried.

"Whatever we do, we'd better do it fast," Ranger said.

Lindsey aimed her camera through the bus window, out at the still-darkening sky.

Flash!

She snapped a few photos and turned to me.

"Damon," Lindsey said, frowning, "I think we may be in trouble."

Lindsey was right. I could see the black cloud getting closer . . . and closer . . .

The gnat cloud was about to swoop down all the way. And if that happened, the bus would get swallowed whole—with us inside!

BURN, BUGGY, BURN

"Everyone off the bus!" the driver said.

Without thinking, I dove for the door. "No!" I said. "We can't go out there!"

"Step back, son," the driver said.

Ranger pulled me back. "Damon," he whispered. "Chill out. Everyone else thinks the gnat cloud is a rain cloud."

The other passengers on the bus gave us funny looks. They all exited the bus with their umbrellas open. They thought rain was on the way.

"Psst! Let's walk to the castle," I whispered to the other three. "It's not that far. Maybe the gnats won't notice if we sneak away."

"Well, *those* gnats won't notice," Stella said. She pointed to the exhaust pipe on the bus. It was stuffed with thousands of dead bugs. Was that why the bus stopped and went out of service? Did the gnats know *we* were on the bus?

I started to walk fast down the road. The squad followed me. The castle was ten minutes away. It only took us five, running as fast as we could. Maybe we really could outsmart the bugs.

When we got to the castle's *Crabzilla* gates, however, a single fly buzzed around the security box. Where one fly flies, more would follow. We didn't have much time.

I rushed to the gate and punched the security code that we'd used last time.

SLIMO.

It didn't work!

SLIMO.

No dice. I looked behind me. The swarm was coming toward us. They had caught up.

Lucky for me, Ranger was right there. He had already figured out what to try next.

MANTIS.

"Same castle, different monster," Ranger quipped. Just like that, the *Crabzilla* claw gates opened.

"Hurry, hurry!" Stella said. "I think the giant gnat cloud is about to make landfall!"

We sprinted to the door and pounded on it.

No answer.

I tried the handle. It was unlocked. We hurried in and slammed the door shut before the bugs could follow us.

"Hello? Anyone home?" I called out. The castle seemed to be deserted.

"We can talk to Walter later," Ranger said. "Let's go to the video vault now!"

We headed downstairs. I hummed the *Mega Mantis* theme song:

Indestructible

Claws and wings

Comes to town to destroy things

Mega-smart! Mega-strong!

Mega-right or Mega-wrong?

Eats you up with just one bite

Mega-Mantis! What a fright!

Stella grabbed my sleeve. "Would you pipe down, you're hurting my ears."

"I'm just having fun!" I said.

"Have fun later," Stella growled. "This is serious."

"Then *seriously* get some earplugs," I said. "Or just go away. Far away."

"Say muenster!" Lindsey cried. I turned and she snapped a picture of us.

The camera flash put a thousand dots in front of my eyes. It was like seeing the backyard fireflies all over again. Thankfully, there were no *real* bugs inside the castle with us—*yet*.

Stella sped up to walk ahead of us. We followed her downstairs and into the video vault. I scanned the walls and shelves and bins and floor and . . .

"Whoa," I said, taking a step back. "Is this place *organized*?"

Movie reels were now lined up alphabetically alongside old video cassettes, DVDs, and other discs.

"Walter said he was going to straighten it out for us," Lindsey said. "I guess he meant it."

"It looks like a real library now," I said excitedly as I glanced over rows and rows of reels. I wondered which ones were originals and which ones were copies.

"Found it!" Stella cried from across the room. Wow! She worked fast!

In Stella's hand was a reel marked *Mega Mantis*.

Ranger noticed there was a sticker on the box, too.

COPY.

We groaned. Something marked *COPY* could not have let loose the giant mantis in Riddle. Only reels marked *ORIGINAL* could be destroyed to stop the monsters. I guess it made sense that Leery would have destroyed all of the originals he had.

"I knew it wouldn't be that easy," Lindsey said. "But let's watch it like we planned and look for some clues."

We popped the reel onto a projector and settled down to watch.

Opening credits scrolled onto the screen. Creepy background music got louder as an ordinary looking praying mantis twitched on a leaf. The camera pulled back to reveal an oversized terrarium and a pair of scientists. They observed the bug through a pair of binoculars. One scientist shouted, "Sir, I think the subject's forelegs are growing again!" The other scientist shouted, "Horrors, my good man!"

These guys were dorkier than the biggest dorks at Riddle Elementary.

All at once, the camera panned to the outside of the scientists' lab. Before I could even think *praying mantis*, the whole building blew up. Just like that, the entire town was blanketed in radioactive isotopic experimental desert dust. Well, that's what some guy in the movie called it.

Leery must have filmed the scenes for *Mantis* out at the old Riddle Air Force hangar. I recognized the wire fence around its borders, the tumbleweeds, and the deserted hangar in the middle of it all. There were these big spotlights that lit everything up, too. What a perfect landing strip for Mega! Where better for a hundred-foot bug to spread its wings?

There were other scenes filmed all over Riddle, too. I recognized the enormous cedar tree that was outside the Riddle Library. Mega snapped off some of its wide branches and chewed them right up. Once Mega Mantis had grown as tall as a skyscraper, it hissed its way through Main Street, stepping on people and animals and destroying every car in sight. The sound effects were incredible!

Ranger and I disagree on many things about the Bs, but one thing we always agree on is that Oswald Leery knew his facts and he used them carefully. If Leery made a movie about bugs, his bugs were mostly anatomically correct and they did bug things. The only monsters with no rules or reality were B-Monsters like the Beast with 1,000 Eyes who could, by the way, *blink* people to death after putting them into zombie trances and making them do very weird things.

But Mega was wild enough for today. We watched as the mantis chomped off someone's head and chewed it like a piece of gum. *Blecch!* Then I noticed something about this B that I had never seen before now: Wherever Mega went, little bugs always surrounded it. Little *swarms* of bugs.

Swarms like the ones that had been following us everywhere.

Near the end of the film, Mega Mantis knocked down an army tank with its forelimbs. Then it scooped up a crowd of unsuspecting bystanders with its power-grip antennae. Nothing—not even a metal tank—was any match for this incredible B-Monster. The entire town was doomed.

But just as Mega was about to crush the tank with a loud hiss, a laser beam shot down from space. Oswald Leery really outdid himself with this movie's special effects. The beam shot down once, then twice, and then a third time.

It was the third ray from space that ignited the

top of Mega's head. In a matter of minutes, the mantis was in full burn. Even its pincers were on fire! Mega Mantis looked more like a birthday candle on top of some cake than a bug. And as it burned, the bug let out this whistling wail. It sent shudders down my spine. Oswald Leery captured the moment perfectly! He shot an ultra-close-up on the mantis's body. It crackled like a barbecued chicken leg on a grill.

"So that's that," I said to the others. "All we need is a space laser."

"A space laser?" Lindsey asked.

"Where are we supposed to get *that*? The space laser *supermarket*?" Stella said sarcastically.

"Um . . . could your dad make a space laser?" I asked, turning to Ranger.

"Yeah, Jesse," Stella said. "Your dad can invent *anything*."

"Gee," Ranger muttered, sounding concerned. "My dad's a pretty busy guy . . ."

"Too busy to save the world?" Lindsey asked.

"Hold on. Maybe we could crisp the giant mantis with something *besides* a laser?" I suggested.

"Like what? A bug-sized flamethrower?" Stella suggested.

"Mega-microwave oven?" I said.

"Mega-nuclear reactor?" Lindsey said.

"How about a plain old pack of mega-matchsticks?" Ranger quipped. "Add a gallon of gasoline and *kaboom*!"

"Um, Damon," Stella said with this intense look on her face, "I don't want to freak you out or anything. But there's something black crawling on your arm . . ."

"Huh?" I jumped up.

"GOTCHA!" Stella cried.

Lindsey and Ranger both laughed.

I gave them both the evil eyeball.

"We need to find Walter and Leery," I grumbled. *"Now."*

THE AMAZE-ING TRUTH

We were all jumpy as we made our way through the castle looking for Walter. Stella kept trying to scare me just for fun. Lindsey kept taking pictures. Every flash made me see double. I had a fear headache. And I didn't want to see another bug. *Ever.*

So when something swooped down past my head, I lost it.

"GIANT INSECT!" I wailed at the top of my lungs.

Only that flying object was no insect. It was Poe the crow, official bird of Leery Castle. He landed on my shoulder. Even though he wasn't nearly as scary as a gnat swarm, my knees were still shaking.

"Hey, Poe. W-w-what's up?" I stammered.

Lindsey giggled. "Photo op!" She held up her camera for a picture. "Say gorgonzola!"

I was ready to scream again, but thankfully Ranger spoke up first. That guy's coolness surprises me sometimes.

"Hey," Ranger suggested. "Maybe Poe can lead us to Walter?"

I looked at the bird. "Yo, Poe, where's Walt?"

Poe let out a *caw* and flew off my shoulder and into the air. We followed him into a long, skinny hallway.

A row of oil paintings hung on the wallpapered walls. The faces all looked like Leery's face, so we guessed these were portraits of Desmond and Lucas Leery, Oswald's father and grandfather. I half expected the pictures to have eyeballs that moved and followed us down the hallway, like the lamest *Scooby Doo* episode ever.

But the eyes didn't move.

Something *else* did.

Each picture was framed in a gold leaf design that looked ordinary from a distance. But up close, I saw the frames were actually made from bugs.

I jumped back.

Then I realized the entire wall was crawling!

I dug around in my pocket for my lucky keychain. It has a penlight on the end of it. I shined the light on to the crawling wall and shivered.

This was so gross.

But there was no time to be scared.

As soon as the pen light hit them, most of the bugs scattered. I saw beetles, grubs, and other crawlies in all sizes. If only I were carrying a portable laser beam instead.

"Geesh," Stella exclaimed. "This place is even bugging *me* out!"

"Everyone run!" I cried, taking off down the hall.

"Wait up!" Ranger called out to me. "Damon! We have to stick together!"

But I sped around a dark corner. I nearly collided with a huge door. Then Stella nearly collided with me.

"What's in there?" Stella asked, reaching for the doorknob.

I clicked my penlight on again. It cast an eerie light in the dark room.

Lindsey and Ranger followed behind us. Lindsey flashed her camera so we could see more inside.

Whoa.

The room was windowless and empty. There wasn't a chair, a table, or even a bulb in the ceiling socket. The floor was scratched and scuffed.

"Creeptastic!" Lindsey said.

"It looks like something was in here," Ranger said, examining the floor. "Bugs?"

"Hmmm . . ." I said.

"Maybe it was something like the Claaaaaw Monster," Stella joked, putting on an evil voice and waving her hand in my face. "I'm coming to claaaaaaw you—"

"Don't say it!" I cowered.

I hate the Claw Monster almost as much as I hate bugs. The Claw only appeared in one Leery movie, but it was one of the scariest Leery films ever. In the movie, the Claw Monster goes from an ordinary hand to a five-fingered monster that no one can control. The Claw has hypnotic powers that convince otherwise ordinary hands to become crazy claws like it is! In the movie, all the hands turn on their humans.

Stella was laughing at me. I'd lost my nerve again and that girl was never going to let me forget it.

"We'd better move!" Ranger said.

"We have a date with Mega!" Stella said. "While we're in here poking around, that bug might be wreaking havoc on our entire town!"

"Gee," I said, "maybe Mega will step on Riddle Elementary and we won't have school tomorrow."

"You say that because you haven't studied for the vocabulary quiz," Stella said.

"I studied more than you did!" I snapped defensively. But that was a big, fat lie. Since the Monster Squad formed, I had barely done my homework. It was tough fighting monsters and cramming for tests at the same time.

"Hey! Over here!" Ranger called out. He found another weird door. "Let's go this way. Maybe we'll find Walter."

The new door led outdoors. We entered a maze of bushes and trees that wound around itself like some kind of snake.

"This is a-maze-ing!" Lindsey called out, chuckling at her own pun.

I recognized a few of the shapes. Crabzilla, Slimo, and Chomp-O were all right here in green leaves.

"Look!" Stella cried. "There's Claw Monster!"

We stopped and stared. The Claw's fingers pointed in a single direction.

Thataway.

The maze path led us into a wide, open, and strangely peaceful space. And there was Walter! He stood at the top of a little ladder, trimming shears in hand.

"We found you!" we all cried at the same time.

"Oh. Hello, kids," Walter said. "Was I lost?"

"Holy guacamole!" Ranger said, pointing up.

I could not believe my eyes. At the center of this enormous topiary maze was the biggest trimmed tree of all.

Mega Mantis.

"Dr. Leery and I have been following your every move," Walter said. He climbed down the ladder.

"You're not the only one following us," Lindsey said, pointing down at the ground.

I froze when I saw what was coming.

Trailing behind us were hundreds of carpenter ants.

And they looked like a real army, ready to attack.

CHAPTER 7

IN DAMON'S ROOM

"Quick, kids!" Walter said, hopping off his ladder. "Follow me."

"No! I'll get 'em!" Stella cried. She started stomping like a maniac.

"Stella, not even a ninja can stomp this many ants," I said, grabbing her arm and pulling her after us.

We retreated to the main part of the castle.

"I can buy us some time," Walter assured us. "Just wait here."

Wait here? Was he kidding?

Ranger, Lindsey, Stella, and I freaked. *The ants were marching one by one, hurrah, hurrah* . . . The song from kindergarten played inside my head.

Then the ants followed us inside.

We hopped up onto a velvet sofa. As the ants

surrounded the claw feet on the sofa, I tried not to panic. But it was impossible to tell where the rug stopped and the ants began.

Then Walter raced back into the room. "Close your eyes!" he commanded.

All at once, I saw a bright flash of green light. Walter held a black stick that looked like a flashlight. He aimed it at the ants.

Zap! Flash! Zap! Flash!

Like magic, the bugs lined up in neat rows.

"How did you get the bugs to *do* that?" Ranger asked.

"Wow," I said. "Can I get a zapper for my little sister?"

Stella shot me one of her serious stares.

"We must contact Dr. Leery right away," Walter went on. "The situation is worse than we anticipated. You need to get instructions directly from him."

I noticed the ant trance was beginning to wear off. The ants were twitching again.

"Oh, dear," Walter cried. "We have to hurry! Head for my limousine! Now!"

The Monster Squad ran out to the car. We flung

ourselves in and buckled up. We had to drive away before the ant trail caught up to us.

As we sped away, Ranger leaned into the front seat. "Where is Leery right now?" he asked. I was wondering the same thing.

"All over the world since last Thursday," Walter explained.

"How does he travel so far so fast?" Stella asked.

"Private B-Jet," Walter answered. "It takes him wherever he goes at a moment's notice."

"So he'll give us instructions from his plane phone?" Lindsey asked.

"No, I just text-messaged him. Dr. Leery wants to stream video to us directly. He recorded a message a short time ago," Walter explained. "Damon, your house is right up here on this road, correct? That is where you saw the insect activity?"

"Sure," I shrugged. "It's a regular Gnat Central."

"Perfect! We'll use your computer for the uplink," Walter told us. "You four can get instructions from Dr. Leery while I investigate Damon's backyard."

As Walter pulled the limo up to my parents' house, I noticed that same empty-neighborhood feeling I'd had the other day. Once again, no one was home. Mom, Dad, and Rachel were probably over at the drive-in getting ready for tonight's show.

As we stepped out of the limo, I glanced up the road.

"Do you see that?" I gushed.

Lindsey screamed.

On the road behind Walter's limousine, where we had just been driving a few moments earlier, was a winding line of ants. The ants from the castle had trailed us from the top of Nerve Mountain!

There was only one difference. The ants were now joined by a moving line of crickets, worms, and slithering slugs.

"Get into the house!" Walter shouted.

I got my key and we raced inside. Stella locked the door behind us.

"Computer?" Walter asked.

I pointed up the stairs. "Top floor."

Stella raced up behind Walter.

I yelled after her. "Don't touch my stuff!" But I knew she was already inside my room.

"Daaaaamon! You have B-Monster posters on the ceiling?" she called out.

"Yes!" I cried. "And on the door, too." I went into the room and found Walter at my computer, punching a bunch of keys.

Lindsey pulled out her camera. "Mind if I snap a few?" she asked me.

I just shrugged. "I guess."

"Where did you get the original poster from the *Crabzilla* premiere?" Ranger asked. "There are only four of those in existence!"

"Yeah," I said. "I got special B souvenirs because of my parents' drive-in. I'm lucky that way."

I quickly showed off all the other B stuff in the room. In addition to posters, I revealed my collection of B-Monster Plushies, trading cards, *B-Monster Galaxy* magazines, an ATTACK OF THE B-MONSTERS game in its original box, and the Slimo paper weight with the hand sticking out of the middle. That had been Leery's too-cool gift for me from our first mission.

Ranger was jealous; I could tell. He probably still thought *he* was the best B-collector in Riddle.

My bedroom curtains were still closed from that morning. I pulled them open so everyone could see the field and forest and maybe even the shadow bug, if he showed up. Drive-O-Rama lights burned bright even though sunset was at least an hour away.

"Okay, Monster Squad," Walter said, getting

up from my computer desk. "No time for playing
around. I've inputted the link to Leery."

Stella squeezed in front of me so she could sit down at the desk.

"Hey," I said, holding back a scream. "That's my computer—"

"While you four chat with Leery," Walter said, "I am going to check out the B-Force levels in your backyard."

"B-Force?" Lindsey asked. "What's that?"

Before we could ask, Walter disappeared downstairs.

My computer hummed as a fuzzy screen came up. A man appeared, like a ghost, through the static.

Oswald Leery!

"My friends," Leery said, clearing his throat. His voice faded in and out. "We meet again. I understand our situation is critical. Walter filled me in on the details. I know you are being swarmed. I also know that Damon has seen a strange and enormous bug in his backyard. I think I have some valuable information for you."

Stella gripped the chair arms. I guess even ninjas get tense, too.

"A few weeks ago," Leery went on, "I learned that the original *Mega Mantis* movie had been screened and a B-Monster had escaped. There were worldwide Mega Mantis sightings. I tracked Mega to Malaysia but then it slipped away!"

We all sucked in a deep breath. Leery adjusted his dark glasses and continued.

"The thing is," Leery explained, "once a B-Monster comes back to life it will always find its way back to Riddle. But Mega Mantis did this sooner than I expected. And once a B-Monster comes back, its powers increase. Mega Mantis gets stronger by the day."

I looked over at Stella. She looked scared.

"But that's not all, Monster Squad!" Leery went on. "You need to know that if a B movie is screened more than once . . . a B may come back to life *more than* once, too."

We all gasped.

"There may be multiple mantids right there in Riddle, right now."

"No way!" I shouted.

"Shhh!" Stella socked me in the arm.

Leery went on.

"Monster Squad," Leery said, "more than one Mega Mantis will invade Riddle in the next twenty-four hours. You four are the only ones who can save our city and the rest of the world. Are you ready?"

CHAPTER 8

WE ARE SO DOOMED

My fists clenched. I could barely imagine one mega-sized praying mantis, let alone *multiple mantids*. And what if the person with the original *Mega Mantis* movie watched it on a video loop? That could mean a zillion mantids on the loose.

"We are SO doomed," I said out loud.

"Yup," Stella said. She rolled her eyes. "Doomed. And that's probably the only time I'll ever agree with you, Molloy."

"Pay attention!" Ranger said, nudging me. Leery was still talking to us through the computer. I pumped up the volume.

"Years ago," Leery explained from behind his dark glasses, "my cameraman shot some research footage in Malaysia. We were able to take incredible photographs of a Mega Mantis loose in the jungle."

Leery flashed us a series of mantis photos. In one picture, the bug was in the process of shedding its skin.

"When a mantis molts," Leery explained, "it becomes more dangerous."

"Eeeeeew," Lindsey said, turning away.

But I stared straight ahead. We had so much to learn about mantids before we could beat these B-Monsters. I didn't want to miss a thing.

Leery went on.

"After these photos were taken, my cameraman vanished. We recovered the camera, but we never located the man . . . or the mantis."

We all let out another gasp.

"I believe that the Mega Mantis in these photographs may have gone back to Riddle. Once he sensed that a new bug had been freed from the original reel, he came to find his brother mantis."

I realized I was shaking. We all were. If what Leery said was true, we were in big trouble. BIG trouble. Fighting Mega Mantis One was bad enough. But fighting a second Mega Mantis? Was that even possible?

"Monster Squad," Leery wheezed, "we cannot

let these creatures destroy Riddle. Are you prepared to fight Mega Mantis and its mates? Prepared for victory? Prepared for triumph?"

"Um, no," I said aloud to the screen.

Stella whacked my shoulder. "Wrong answer, lame-o," she said. "Of course we're ready!"

"I know you must have questions," Leery said. "If my calculations are correct, an instant-messaging program should appear on your desktop right now . . ."

All at once, a small box popped up on the screen.

Please type your questions here. I'll do my best to answer.

He'd timed it perfectly! It was the first time we'd get to talk to Leery in person. Of course, Stella typed first. She always hogs all the best moments.

Why r sooo many other bugs flying around Riddle near MegaM?

Stella hit ENTER and sat back. A response came quickly. We were talking to the real, live Leery!

B-Monsters have a tremendous B-Force.

I wanted to ask something else, but Stella typed again.

What's B-Force?

Leery replied.

B-Force is the chemical power of attraction between a monster and its environment. The B-Force around Mega Mantis is bugs. If there are many bugs swarming, you know the B is close. If a swarm suddenly vanishes, the B has flown away. But it will always come back. So will its B-Force. B-ware!!!!

"Hey! Walter was just talking about B-Force!" I cried. "Remember? He was headed out to the backyard to measure it."

"This sure explains the growing gnat cloud," Ranger said.

"And the ants at the castle!" Stella added.

"And the other insects that followed us here!" Lindsey said.

I gulped, suddenly realizing what all this meant. "Mega Mantis is closer than we think."

"But *which* Mega Mantis?" Ranger asked. "One or two?"

Another message from Leery popped up.

B-Force is usually seen only by people who can see the monsters but sometimes the force is so strong that others may witness swarms or clusters. When a

B-Monster has reached maximum power and is about to strike, everyone will see the B-Force bugs.

We stared at the monitor. Ranger leaned over Stella and typed.

So what do we do now???

We waited.

To beat the B-Monster, you need to strike when the time is right. Chances are that the mantids will disappear to shed their skins. When they reappear, they will be ready to battle you. Learn everything you can about the real mantids, including how to destroy them. With the right knowledge, the Monster Squad can and will defeat any B-Monster.

Without warning, our instant-messaging box closed. The screen went back to gray static.

"Where did Leery go?" I pushed Stella out of the way and punched at my keyboard. "How can a few online searches help us fight one massive B-bug? This is nuts!"

"You mean *gnats*?" Lindsey giggled.

"Let's review the facts," Stella declared. "We're facing more than one Mega Mantis. And we already know each bug is as tall as the screen at the Drive-O-Rama! This really is nuts."

"You mean GNATS!" Lindsey said again.

"Look. We have a job to do," Ranger said. "We made a promise to Leery and we have to keep that promise."

Stella turned back to my computer and took over again. She typed:

PRAYING MANTIS BUG BIG MONSTER

She got 11,473 hits.

Ranger leaned over her shoulder and began scrolling through a list of web links. He clicked on ETYMOLOGY OF ENTYMOLOGY.

Etymology is the study of words. Entymology is the study of insects! This site just for kids has both! Click on a bug name to find out its real meaning.

We looked over the list of bug names and clicked on MANTIS.

Mantis comes from the Greek word for prophet or fortune teller. Mantids are named for their "prayer-like" stance.

"Yeah," I quipped, "like we better pray they don't eat us!"

When a mantis is threatened, some species may be aggressive toward one another. They can turn into cannibals.

"Um . . . don't cannibals *eat* one another?" I said.

"Haven't you ever wanted to bite off your friend's head?" Lindsey joked.

I walked away from the computer and flopped down on my bed. I was losing my nerve again. I couldn't do this.

"Whoa!" Stella cried out a moment later. "Is that a mantis," she gasped, "with a *man* in his mouth?"

"What?" I said, sitting up. "What are you looking at?"

"That looks like our science teacher, Mr. Bunsen," Ranger cried.

"Huh? No way," I said, pushing my way over to see the screen. "Let me see what you're looking—"

"Gotcha again!" Stella said.

Ranger and Lindsey gave each other a high five.

When the three of them laughed at me, I was ready to squash them *all* like bugs.

CHAPTER 9

MEGA
MEGA

Who knew there were so many web pages about mantids?

There were blogs and guides from bug doctors, people who worked in zoos, and even students like us. There was even a SUPER MANTIS roller coaster. Someday I'll have to visit *that* theme park.

I tore out a sheet of paper and made a list of our facts.

What We Know About the Mantis So Far

Hunts and snatches things
Very fast!!!
Hisses
Camouflaged during both day and night
Rocks from side to side

Sheds its skin, but just before shedding, it does not eat. After shedding, all it wants to do is eat.

Awake in the daytime (diurnal) but also goes for bright lights at night

"I wish I had the power to camouflage myself or change into something other than me," I said.

"What? Like a bug?" Stella cracked.

"Funny," I grumbled. I tried to change the subject. "Is anyone thirsty?"

"Yeah," Ranger said. "Got any bug juice?"

"QUIT IT!" I barked. I wasn't going to let these losers tease *me*.

But Lindsey and Stella just cracked up.

"Go ahead and laugh!" I said. I walked out and headed for the sliding doors. I wondered what Walter had been doing in the backyard all this time.

But when I opened the drapes, it was pitch-black.

"Huh? Hey, Ranger! What time is it?" I called out.

"Five forty-two," Ranger yelled back. "Why?"

"You guys better get down here," I cried.

The girls ran to the window first. "Ewwwww!" they cried in unison. "BUGS!"

They were right, of course. The window was

smothered with wings and gummy little bodies. Everything oozed so thick it blocked the remaining daylight.

Where had they come from?

"We should look outside and see what's going on!" Stella cried. She ran for the door first.

"Wait!" I yelled. "Mega Mantis is probably out there!"

"Exactly," Stella said.

Ranger and Lindsey followed Stella to the back door.

"Um," I called out, "I think I'll stay inside. Just in case."

"Come on," Ranger said, tugging my sleeve. "We're in this together, remember? You can do this."

I took a breath and followed the other three.

We looked up at the house to see a massive blanket of bugs spread out across the entire second floor. Bugs blocked *all* the windows at 18 Cicada Lane.

And Walter was nowhere to be found!

"Do you hear that?" Lindsey asked. She grabbed my arm.

The noise sounded like two sticks rubbing together, only way louder.

"I hear it!" Stella declared.

"There!" Ranger said, pointing to the edge of the field.

"I'll investigate," Stella announced. And before we had a chance to stop her, she slipped into the high grass. A moment after she went in, we lost sight of her.

"Stella?" I called out loudly. "Come back!"

I expected her to jump right back out of the field. It would be another one of her "Gotcha!" moments.

But Stella didn't reappear.

"This is just some kind of Stella trap," I said. "I go in after her; she scares the macaroni salad out of me. You know the drill."

"But what if she *isn't* setting a trap?" Ranger asked.

"What if Mega Mantis found her?" Lindsey asked.

Chi-chi-chi-chuuuuuut.

We all froze.

"What was *that*?" Lindsey asked.

That noise wasn't coming from the direction of the field. It was coming from the direction of the house. We turned around, *slowly*.

Mega Mantis was right behind us. It was way more mega than I could have *ever* imagined.

The giant mantis stood between us and the house like some great, armored tank. It had sharp pincers and bulbous eyes with bumps on them. Mega's body was dark green and speckled with bug scars—or at least they looked like scars. This mantis had done battle before. It must have been the mantis from the jungle! Slimy, blue drool dripped off its fangs into puddles on the ground as it stood there, twitching madly. It raised its antennae high in the air, listening.

To us?

"Let's get out of here!" I panicked. We all panicked.

"What about Stella?" Lindsey cried. She turned toward the field.

"And Walter!" Ranger said. "We have to find them both."

We looked up at the roof. The gnats on the house windows had lifted into another enormous black cloud. The larger swarm hovered around Mega's head. It was just like the school bus cloud and the Nerve Mountain cloud—only *much* bigger!

"We have to go!" Lindsey yelled at me.

We ran into the field. But where were we running to? Stella was missing. Walter was missing. My arm was . . . *itching*?

I looked down and saw a cluster of furry caterpillars crawling up my arms and legs. They were all over Ranger and Lindsey, too. It was Leery's B-Force–times ten! The B-Force had gotten stronger when Mega came into the yard.

"More bugs?" Ranger cried.

"Drop to the ground!" Lindsey said. "Treat it like a fire. Stop, drop, and roll!"

There was no time to think. We fell down flat and wriggled around on the ground. I couldn't get those furballs off me fast enough.

A moment later, we were up on our feet

again, running deeper into the grassy field. I couldn't see anything or anyone.

Squeeeeeeeeeeeee.

Now Mega Mantis was coming! What would he do to us?

Thwack.

I fell backward onto the ground and rubbed my head. It took me a minute before I realized that I'd collided headfirst into another person.

"Stella?"

Her eyes were wild. She and Walter had been

hiding out in the grass together. They both looked so scared.

"Did you kids see Mega Mantis?" Walter asked.

"Uh," I said, "it's a hundred feet tall. Kind of hard to miss . . ."

"And it's not alone!" Stella gasped.

"What?" Lindsey cried.

I clutched my chest.

"Leery was right," Stella

said. "There are at least *three* Mega Mantids in the field. And there are probably more in Riddle."

"More? How is that possible?" Ranger asked.

"I saw a pile of mantis skins out there!" Stella cried.

We all knew that when a praying mantis shed its skin, the skin looked just like the creature. Even its eyes and mouth were preserved. That was one photograph Lindsey couldn't resist. She pulled out her camera and headed in the direction of the skins.

"Stick together!" Walter said.

All at once, a sonic booming noise shook the ground. We hit the dirt.

Va-vroooooooooom.

Something sped over our heads. It was like a jetliner, only louder.

"WHAT'S HAPPENING NOW!?" I screamed.

We lay there, stunned. Then, just as quickly as it boomed, the air got very still.

"Did I dream it, or did Mega Mantis just fly over our heads?" Lindsey asked.

"Not just one mantis," Walter said. "Three!"

"Three?" I said. My voice quavered.

"But where did they go?" Stella asked.

"And when will they be back?" I cried.

"We have to wait," Walter instructed.

"Here?" Lindsey asked.

"No, go back home. I'll head back to the castle. This will take some time. Go to school tomorrow. The mantids will show up again when they're hungry," Walter explained.

"Hungry?" we all said at the exact same time.

"Of course!" I cried. "Remember what Leery said? We have to do our homework. We need to research the bugs and learn how to fight them *before* the big attack."

Stella gave me a look. "Since when did you get so smart?" she cracked.

I puffed out my chest.

"Since I joined Monster Squad," I said.

HELLO, PRINCIPAL PICKLE

Pat and Seamus gave me the cold shoulder at lunch the next day. I knew why. I sat with the Monster Squad instead of them—*again*.

But I didn't have a choice. Once this B-Monster thing started, there was no splitting us up. We stuck together when we fought Slimo and that worked great. Why should now be any different?

Since the Mega sighting in the field near the Drive-O-Rama, there had been no new signs of the mantis or its friend, Mega Mantis Two. But we just kept waiting, like Walter said we should. No news should have been good news. But it wasn't. The bugs were all we could think about.

"Let's break it down," Stella said, poking at her plate of mashed potatoes. "The mantids flew away. But Leery told us they always come back.

90

We have to figure out *where* they'll show up next."

Lindsey took a bite of salad. She'd nearly drowned it in ranch dressing.

I pushed my fork through the ziti on my plate. But I wasn't really hungry.

Who could eat that at a time like this?

"Molloy!" Ranger cried, waving his hands at me. "What's that on your plate?"

"Pasta, bro," I said, holding up a forkful.

"Mmmm, I don't think so . . ." Ranger said.

I dropped my fork with a clang. These weren't ziti tubes! There were wriggling *larvae* on my tray!

"Yo, Ranger!" I winced. "*You* have bugs, too . . ."

"Smother them in Lindsey's ranch dressing," Ranger cried. He grabbed Lindsey's salad plate and dumped it on the larvae.

But Lindsey's plate had bugs of her own!

"Ewwww!" Lindsey said. "I thought those little black things were seeds. They're ants!"

Stella looked down at her plate and nudged a lettuce leaf. From underneath the salad, a line of beetles marched from the plate onto the tray.

"UGH!" Stella squealed. "I ATE LIVE BUGS, TOO! GROSS!"

Normally, Stella Min shoulda, coulda, and most definitely woulda handled herself like a cool and calm ninja. But today she stood right up and flipped out. In fact, she flipped her entire lunch tray. Her plate sailed off our table into

the back of an unfortunate student with an even more unfortunate name.

"Beef!" I cried.

This was not good.

Beef grunted and stood up. Stella's food

dripped down his back. But he looked right at *me* and growled.

"You did this?"

One of Beef's friends sneered at me and hurled a dish of pudding at my head. I ducked and it hit Ranger in the shoulder. Some splattered on Lindsey.

There was no turning back now.

The food fight was on.

It took a few minutes for security to arrive. But by then, the entire lunchroom was one splattered canvas of potatoes, ketchup, turkey slices, orange peels, chocolate chip cookie crumbs, spaghetti sauce, and pink yogurt.

Somehow, we got the blame for starting it.

"I'll see you four instigators downstairs," growled Security Guard Spiker.

"What are we supposed to do *now*?" Lindsey asked as we shuffled down the hall.

"Maybe Mega Mantis will attack the school and we'll get out of being punished," I said. I was only half kidding.

Spiker sat us down on a row of hard, wooden chairs outside Principal Pickle's office.

"Wait here and don't move a muscle," Spiker said.

"But this stinks," I mumbled.

"That includes mouth muscles!" Spiker snapped.

As soon as Spiker walked away, Lindsey panicked.

"They're going to call our parents!" she blubbered. "Dad will take my camera away. He always does that when he gets angry."

I glanced up at the clock. "Maybe it's not so bad," I said. "If we have to sit here for the entire next period, I'll miss that vocabulary test."

"You'll just have to retake it tomorrow," Ranger said.

"Why aren't we talking about the *bugs*?" Stella said. She made a fist and pounded the inside of her palm. "The B-Force is back. We have a job to do!"

"Mega Mantis is getting close again," Ranger said. "That can't be good."

Just then, the principal came out. He had on a dark green pin-striped suit. His name was Pickle and he looked like one, too.

"Hello, Principal Pickle," we said, lowering our heads and trying to look sorry.

"I am very disappointed," Principal Pickle said. "I phoned your parents. They should be here any minute. Why don't you wait in the other office?"

The principal shuffled us into an empty room and shut the door.

Lindsey looked miserable. "I told you this would happen!" she said, collapsing onto a chair.

"Everyone remain calm," Ranger said, pacing. "We're not in any big trouble yet."

"I'm not in big trouble *ever*!" Stella crossed her arms. "I didn't even participate in that stupid food fight anyway!"

"Wait one minute," I growled. "*You* threw the first lunch tray, Stella Min. So don't go playing Miss Innocent, because you're guilty just like the rest of us."

Stella's face dropped. Lindsey and Ranger looked stunned, too.

"We're in this together, right?" I said to everyone. "That means good and bad, right?"

"You're right," Lindsey said. She lifted her camera up to take my photograph. "Say cheddar, Damon!"

I made a face.

The room fell silent for a moment, until Lindsey cracked, "So what's up with the principal's pickle suit?"

We all chuckled at that one. Even Stella was grinning.

Then the door swung open.

"I hope you aren't laughing at this situation, students," Principal Pickle said. I spotted my dad standing just behind him. Ranger's dad was there, too, next to Stella's and Lindsey's mothers.

"Your parents and I agree," Principal Pickle declared, "that the four of you can return to classes as normal for the rest of the day, but you will report to the school cafeteria lunch staff to help serve and clean for one full week."

I imagined being up to my elbows in a vat of our school's superglue mashed potatoes. Could there be any worse torture than that?

The girls took off with their moms. Ranger and I faced our dads.

"I'm sorry, Dad," Ranger started to say. His dad interrupted.

"Jesse, I think you learned a valuable lesson here, don't you?" his dad said.

"Indeed," my dad piped up. "Never start a food fight, unless you can't get caught!"

Both dads laughed hard. Ranger and I just rolled our eyes. *Welcome to Embarrassment City,* I thought to myself. Then I got an idea. I turned to Ranger's dad.

"Mr. Ranger, you're a scientist, right?" I said. "Well, can you answer a scientific question?"

"I will certainly try," Ranger's dad said to me.

"Can mantids grow to be extra large?" I asked.

"Extra large?" Mr. Ranger said, laughing. "What? Like Mega Mantis?"

My dad laughed even louder. "Do you watch

those old flicks, Ranger? Damon loves B-Monsters, don't you, son?"

Ranger and I shifted uncomfortably.

"Seriously, Dad," Ranger butted in. "Can mantids attack people for real?"

"Gee," Ranger's dad said thoughtfully, "I know of only one *real* Giant Mantis attack. It took place in a

remote village in . . . Malaysia, I think. A colleague of mine told me about it once . . ."

Malaysia? That was where Leery had last seen Mega!

"Why the sudden interest in insects, boys?" my dad asked. "Damon, I thought you hated bugs . . ."

"Yeah, well," I turned back to Ranger's dad. "Who was that colleague you mentioned?"

"Name is Dr. Von Rosenhof. And I do believe he just returned from a research trip. He has studied mantids extensively throughout his career."

"Really?" This sounded like a guy we needed to meet.

"Believe it or not, Dr. Von Rosenhof lives right here in Riddle, right up the road from the school," Ranger's dad added.

"That's a coincidence!" my dad chuckled.

Ranger flashed me a look. I knew exactly what he was thinking.

This was no coincidence.

It was a clue!

CHAPTER 11

SQUAD FOR ONE, SQUAD FOR ALL

It took all my strength to get through the rest of the school day. After our temporary detention, I had to take that vocabulary quiz. What a bust. I didn't recognize half the words.

When the end-of-day bell rang, I met up with the others at our lockers. Our dads had given us a major clue. We had new information and we had to adjust our plan of action. The four of us headed to the library to look up Dr. Von Rosenhof's address in Riddle. We found it in the white pages. Stella recognized the street and house number right away.

"I know exactly where he lives!" Stella said. "You can't really see the house from the road because of this tall fence but he has these bright spotlights on the property."

"Okay," Ranger asked. "What now?"

"Let's go to Von Roffenfoffer's place!" I cried.

Stella knuckle-noogied my shoulder. "It's Von Rosenhof, Molloy. If you can't even get his name right . . ."

"Von Rosenhoof, Von Foofenpoof," I groaned. "What difference does it make? We wouldn't even *have* his name if I hadn't asked Dr. Ranger . . ."

"Let's call! Stella, you have a cell phone," Ranger said.

Stella dialed his phone number, but no one picked up. Not even an answering machine.

"So *now* what?" Lindsey said.

"Plan B," I said.

"We're already on Plan B, Molloy," Stella moaned. "Enough planning. Let's pounce!"

"Stella's right. We should figure out a way to beat the bugs on our own," Lindsey said. "Just in case Dr. Von Rosenhof doesn't turn up before we have to face them."

"What about using one of those zappers Walter had at the castle?" Ranger suggested. "We could zap the bugs into a radioactive coma."

"I don't think zappers are what we need," Stella

said. "We need explosives! Let's blast the bugs into bits."

"And blast ourselves, too?" Ranger said.

"Have we completely given up on the space laser thing?" I asked.

"That's it!" Lindsey cried. "We don't have a real space laser but we could invent a bug weapon of our own."

"We can certainly try," Ranger said. "My dad's laboratory is open. He has a bunch of tools and supplies we could use."

"After we do that, we need to lure the bugs somewhere," Stella said.

"We can totally lure them. This is a great plan!" Lindsey cried.

Everyone lifted their palms for a group high five. On contact, Ranger pulled his hand away and wiped it on his pants. He looked right at me.

"Damon, what is wrong with your hand?"

I looked down. My hand was so super-duper sweaty, it was dripping.

"That's disgusting, Molloy!" Stella cried, shaking her own hand out.

Lindsey smiled at me. "*Really* disgusting. Good one."

"Squad for one and squad for all!" I fake-cheered.

If only my clammy palms could defeat Mega Mantis. Then we'd *really* be in business.

CHAPTER 12

BUG
VS.
BUG

For someone who couldn't stand the sight of a fly one week earlier, I was getting used to the B-Force bugs.

Dr. V would have been really helpful right about now. He could have lectured us on the weaknesses of the average mantis. But he still wasn't answering his phone and we didn't want to show up at his place unannounced. It wasn't like Leery Castle, where we knew we were welcome to just walk in and snoop around.

Instead, we headed for Ranger's dad's laboratory. When we parked our bikes outside, I noticed lots of spiders around the place. I guess B-Force attracts eight-legged creatures the same way it attracts six-legged ones.

Mr. Ranger's lab was full of amazing stuff. He's

working on a special machine that can wash your clothes while you're still wearing them. I don't really understand how that's possible, but it sure sounded cool.

Mr. Ranger wasn't around; Jesse gave us the grand tour.

"What are we looking for?" Lindsey asked.

"Helpful gadgets," Stella said.

"Like this?" Lindsey held up an oversized swatter. "S'wat do you think, Damon?"

"Buzz off!" I joked back.

Everyone laughed except for Stella. She was in one of her serious moods.

Bins and buckets were crammed into every corner of Mr. Ranger's lab. Objects had been neatly stored and labeled in bold letters.

BOLTS

CLASPS

PUMPS

But the whole place wasn't just bits and pieces. There were some old or non-working inventions piled up around the place, too. Like the Amazing Electric Melter, an eggbeater that sent out heat rays! Could this melt bugs? Probably not. It was way too small to fry even the most miniscule mantis.

I found a fifty-foot Rope-O-Matic buried under some boxes. Ranger said it was a tape measure for cowboys. Instead of tape inside, it had enough rope to lasso a bull.

"Let's lasso Mega Mantis!" I suggested.

Stella thought it was a fun idea, but we agreed it would be tough to rope all six bug legs at once.

In a far corner of Mr. Ranger's lab, Lindsey found something that would work. She spotted a stash of spray cans with hoses still attached. They looked a little like water guns, only with bigger barrels and buttons all over.

These had potential. I grabbed a couple.

"I remember those!" Ranger said. "They were supposed to shrink things but Dad could never make them work. He could never come up with the right formula."

"Shrinking potion sounds cool," I said thoughtfully. "But I have another idea. If we can't shrink 'em, let's squirt 'em!"

I'd already spotted the poison: RID.

Everyone knew RID was the go-to poison for rats,

bugs, fungus, and lots of other gross stuff. My mom kept some locked up under our sink. It was marked *extremely dangerous* but I knew it was *exactly* what the Monster Squad needed to beat this B-Monster.

"We can pour the RID into the discarded spray cans!" Ranger said.

"If we spray enough at the exact same time," Lindsey said, "we can stun the mantids. Those bugs won't know what hit 'em."

I opened up the cans so we could pour in the RID. It smelled so bad, like wet dog. But we managed to fill two cans each with the stuff. Mr. Ranger would have freaked out if he saw us handling these hazardous materials. But we carefully put on gloves and safety masks that we also found in the lab.

In no time we were armed and ready to take down some bad bugs. Our specially rigged backpacks were ready. Whoever spotted Mega Mantis first was supposed to yell, "SPRAY!" Then we'd all shoot at the target.

"Let's go over Molloy's list again," Ranger said. He took a pencil from his dad's lab desk and made notes. We needed to use the information we'd gathered so far. It would help us to figure out where to look for Mega and its pals next.

What We Know About the Mantis So Far

Hunts and snatches things—like us???
Very fast!!!—can even FLY!!!
Hisses—makes loud squeeeeee before appearing. Very loud.
Camouflaged during both day and night—except for the fact that it is as big as a tour bus!!!

Rocks from side to side—have not seen this

Sheds its skin, but just before shedding, it does not eat. After shedding, all it wants to do is eat—Stella SAW skins; they are real. Do we go back to the field???

Awake in the daytime (diurnal) but also goes for bright lights at night

"Wait! Reread the last one!" Lindsey said. "The mantids are diurnal. That has to be the clue we need."

"But it can't be the right clue," I said. "It's not diurnal anymore. It's nighturnal."

"Nocturnal," sneered Stella.

Night. Noct. Dark was coming fast.

I was beginning to wonder if we'd missed our chance to get the bugs until daylight tomorrow.

"Wait!" I put a finger into the air. "What if the mantids can be fooled by *fake* bright light? Like the ones in Dr. Vanfoofenpoof's yard?"

The other three stared at me like I was dense, but I knew exactly what I was talking about.

"Damon," Stella moaned. "Those aren't that big. Where can we possibly find enough fake light to trick three giant mantids in Riddle?"

"The Drive-O-Rama!" I cried.

CHAPTER 13

BUG TORNADO

As we left Mr. Ranger's laboratory, the last bit of daylight faded from the sky. But we were still on the hunt for Mega Mantis One and the others.

The Drive-O-Rama's bright lights would be flickering on right about now, so we had to hurry. We wanted to get the bugs, destroy them, and then find the owner of the original reel and destroy that, too.

That was a lot of homework for one night, but we were on the move!

It was tough riding our bikes over to the Drive-O-Rama with those mammoth-sized packs on our back, but we did it. We came up over a small bluff and spotted the neon sign: *Drive-O-Rama*. The lights at the drive-in were as bright as baseball stadium lights. Mega Mantis couldn't resist this place.

111

Time for the main event.

We staked out the main area of the drive-in and waited to see who would show up. Ordinary people packed the drive-in tonight, but there were no signs of any Mega Mantis.

All we could do was wait.

"Hey!" I cried out. "Something just stung me!"

"Me too!" Lindsey said, thwacking her arm.

RIDDLE
Drive-O-Rama

TONIGHT'S SCREENING
MEGA MANTIS

We'd been so busy rushing around to get to the Drive-O-Rama that we didn't notice the swarm was back. It was bigger than ever.

I slapped Ranger's back—hard. "Yee-ouch!" he yelled. "What did you do that for?"

"There was a moth the size of my palm on your back!" I said. Then I realized that I'd touched bug goo with my bare hand. I couldn't wipe it off fast enough on my jeans.

"Back off, bugs!" Stella yelled at the swarm, trying to stomp and shoo at the same time. "Kiiiiiiya!"

Why did she think that a karate kick was the answer to everything?

"We'll be eaten alive before Mega Mantis even shows up," Ranger said.

All at once, I heard a loud snap.

Out of nowhere, a cold gust of wind blew past us.

Whooooooosh!

The bugs around us got sucked up into the air like they were being picked up by the world's largest vacuum cleaner. A tornado of insects whipped across the parking lot.

I saw where they were headed.

"Over there! It's here!" I screamed. "Mega Mantis One!"

Mega Mantis One was as big, green, and mean as it had been in my backyard. Its battle scars glinted in the Drive-O-Rama lights. It looked like a B-Monster, but this bug was real. It opened its pincers like it was about to strike.

Then, without warning, a *second* mantis crash-landed nearby! Mega Mantis Two raised its front arms and hissed loudly. It looked just like Mega Mantis One, except that it didn't have as many scars.

Squeeeeeeeeeeeeeeee.

"Ack!" I said, covering my ears.

I scanned the parking lot. Why didn't other people here see what we saw? Some just sat in their cars like statues. Others strolled over to the Drive-O-Rama Snack Shack as if everything were normal. Kids played on the swings located underneath the giant drive-in screen. Didn't anyone notice the fifty-foot bugs with the blue drool? Wasn't the B-Force big enough yet? What did it take for ordinary people to see Mega?

"Unbelievable!" Ranger pointed up at the dark

sky. There, in the middle of the blue-black, Mega Mantis Three flew into view! It circled overhead like a bird.

Mega Mantis One knew Three was there, though. One reared on its four back legs.

Hisssssssssss.

Stella reared back on *her* two legs and struck a ninja pose. "We need to fire our spray cans—*now*!"

"We can't!" I cried. "If we shoot RID at the drive-in, we'll poison all the people!"

"And that would be bad," Lindsey said.

Mega Mantis Two moved toward Mega Mantis One. They were grinding their cannibal jaws. I knew what that meant. They were hungry for each other and probably for us, too.

Then the bug cyclone whisked back into view. It was twice its previous size and whirling toward us.

"We have to run!" I cried.

Backpacks on, we ran to safer ground near the Snack Shack. The sound of trumpets blared over the Mega hissing and the swarm buzz. All at once, the very bright Drive-O-Rama lights dimmed.

"Oh no! The movie is starting!" I cried.

"What are your parents showing tonight?" Ranger asked.

Up on-screen, the title appeared in bold letters.
MEGA MANTIS
Starring G. W. Stinx and Sandra Lee

"I forgot all about the movie schedule!" I cried. "And I just checked it yesterday! How could I have forgotten to tell you guys?"

"What else did you forget to tell us?" Stella moaned.

"Hey!" Lindsey shouted. "Maybe the Drive-O-Rama has the original reel?"

"Good thought," I said, but I shook my head. "Unfortunately Dad ditched most of his reels last year. He uses DVDs now."

"That's still some crazy coincidence," Ranger said, chuckling.

"Yeah," I said, looking up at a giant bug on the screen. I would have laughed, too, if I wasn't about to get body-slammed by one of the giant bugs in the parking lot.

Rrrrrarrrrrrkkkkk!

Mega Mantis One and Mega Mantis Two moved toward each other like freight cars out of control.

They made the ground shake so much, I thought it would split open. The bugs collided, legs thrashing. With one low swoop, Mega Mantis One leaned in and opened its jaws wide. Then *cruuuunch.*

One bit off Two's head!

"Eeeeeeew!" we all yelled.

Lindsey snapped a photo just as Mega Mantis One spit out the head.

Bleeeech! I thought I was going to throw up.

The large mantis head bounced into the parking lot like a volleyball from Coach Dunne's gym class. The headless bug body crumpled to the ground.

Up on-screen, *Mega Mantis* the movie finally began. Mega Mantis One turned to the screen and raised his front legs like he was about to attack. He thought the movie mantis was real!

B-Force spun through the parking lot, whipping up dirt and grass and litter off the ground. I saw some ordinary people acting differently. Couples rolled up their car windows. Kids let out squeaks and screams. It was just like what Leery had said. If the B-Force was strong enough . . .

Everyone would see the bugs.

The Drive-O-Rama had become Chaos-O-Rama.

Thankfully, the crowds of people only saw the bug tornado. If they'd seen Mega Mantis and the other enormous mantids, who knows what would have happened?

The Monster Squad watched as headless Mega Mantis Two staggered into the field next to the drive-in. Mega Mantis One turned away from the movie screen and raised his large front legs. Something was coming. His antennae stood straight up.

Rrrrrrarrrrrrrkkkkk!

Out of nowhere, Mega Mantis Three swooped down and crash-landed on Mega Mantis One. Their combined screeches sounded like a bunch of dolphins with the volume turned all the way up. I thought my ears would explode.

Sqweeeeeeeeeee.

"Damon? Damon, is that *you*?"

Somehow, I heard a voice calling me through all the noise.

Mom?

"Damon! Thank goodness you're all right," Mom said. "What's happening? Where did all these bugs come from?"

"Um . . . um . . ." I was completely speechless. Was I supposed to tell her the *truth*?

"Have you seen Rachel?" Mom cried. "She was with us in the Snack Shack and then she vanished . . ."

Vroooooooooom.

I glanced up as Mega Mantis One and Mega Mantis Three took off like airplanes. The downdraft nearly blew us over. We ducked as the massive bugs zipped around in a loop-dee-loop formation. Then they landed back near the Drive-O-Rama screen. They were still drawn to the too-bright screen light and the movie mantis!

Mom looked a little bit panicked, but she only seemed worried about the little bugs. Thankfully she could not see any of the Mega B-Monsters . . . yet.

"Mom, maybe you should go back into the Snack Shack and look for Rachel," I suggested. "I'll look out here."

"Okay, but hurry," Mom said. "The TV says there's a big storm coming. We have to find your little sister!" She ran back to the Snack Shack.

I glanced at the parking lot. Or what was left of

it. There was a shrill scream we heard above the rest of the commotion.

"HELP ME!"

"Molloy! On the ladder!" Ranger said, pointing. "It's your sister!"

I couldn't believe my eyes. Rachel was climbing up the side of the Drive-O-Rama movie screen and she was stranded on the ladder.

"Rachel! Don't move!" I yelped.

It looked like Mega Mantis One and Mega Mantis Three were about to have her for a Mega snack.

CHAPTER 14

STOMPTACULAR

"Don't worry! I'll save you!" I cried out.

I ran toward the movie screen. Ranger tried to stop me.

"Hey, man, I think maybe we need to slow down, you know, because these bugs aren't so friendly and well, what if the mantids try to . . . eat *you*?"

"No!" I insisted, climbing onto the bottom rung of the ladder. "I have to save her!" I threw the pack off my back and started up.

"Go, Damon, go!" Lindsey cheered after me. She had her camera up and snapping. *Gulp*. I hoped these wouldn't be the last pictures ever taken of Rachel or me.

As I climbed toward her, Rachel looked so scared. Then I realized something pretty important.

Rachel saw Mega Mantis One and Mega Mantis Three. She *saw* them. But how?

As I reached her sneakers, I turned. My stomach flip-flopped. Both mantids were close enough to swallow us in one gulp.

"Get away from us!" I screamed. Every part of me was shaking.

So why weren't the giant mantids attacking?

Neither Mega Mantis seemed to notice that I was within chomping distance. They turned their heads around 180 degrees and moved into the field.

"Are you okay?" Lindsey cried. She was still taking photos. I saw her flash go off.

"Where are they going?" Stella shouted from below the ladder. "Can you see from up there?"

"I think the Mega Mantids are headed for Riddle Air Base," I yelled down, following them with my eyes.

"Of course!" Stella yelled. "The hangar! It's home! Bright lights! Lots of space! Just like Leery's movie!"

Rachel was just above me now. She was a quivering mass of Jell-O, too. I reached up and grabbed her hand. Then we went back down the ladder together.

"You saved my life!" Rachel gushed once we stepped onto the ground.

"Yeah, well, *duh*," I said and tried to play it cool. "I'm not just going to stand there and do nothing. Mom would ground me forever."

"I swear on a stack of *B-Monster Galaxy*

magazines that I'll never, ever laugh at you again," Rachel said.

"Don't get carried away," I grumbled.

Stella raced over to us. She handed me my pack back.

"We have to go to the Air Force Base!" she yelled. "Now!"

I looked at my sister. "Rachel, what did you see up there?" I whispered.

"Everything," Rachel whispered back. "The little bugs. And the big bugs, too. I saw one in our backyard, too, the other day. I know I should have told you. But it was way more fun watching you be scared."

I was dumbfounded. I couldn't believe she'd seen it all. Was she one of *us*?

"We have to talk later," I told her. "But right now go straight to the Snack Shack and find Mom."

I raced across the field and followed the rest of the Monster Squad to the hangar.

When we came up to the air hangar, something was humming. I looked around and spotted the generator for the big lights on the runway. Those lights went on every night like clockwork.

The runway was an emergency landing strip for the area.

Stella saw something else in the grass. "Look!" she cried. "It's glowing!"

There on the edge of the field was the headless body of Mega Mantis Two. Next to it were more Mega Mantis skins.

Finding the skins, of course, seemed pretty cool right then. But it was actually not a good thing. Skins meant that the mantids were here and ready to fight. They were probably ready to destroy our entire town and the rest of the world until they ate everything and everyone and burped away life as we knew it.

The Monster Squad couldn't let that happen.

"Fire on sight," Ranger ordered like some kind of major general.

I shifted my pack to make sure all my cans were ready to spray. They were so heavy. My back was killing me.

"Look! More mantids!" Lindsey cried.

I squinted into the light. I spotted Mega Mantis One and Mega Mantis Three, and then I freaked.

There were five *more* bugs, and they were all getting

ready to fight one another from the looks of it! A fight like that would destroy Riddle. Which meant that we had to kill seven mantids at once! Impossible!

Their mouths were hanging wide open. Fangs dripped with blue drool.

"Ready?" Stella howled at the top of her lungs.

We steadied our cans and hoses.

"Aim . . ."

I held my breath and braced myself.

"SPRAY!"

Those B-Monster bugs didn't know what hit them. The spray gushed out of all our hoses in a powerful burst. The formula seemed to sting the bugs. They made that noise like at the drive-in.

Squeeeeeeeeeee.

One hose worked fine. But when I went to reload, it jammed. I was stuck with a bad can. I reached around to my backpack to fix it, when I saw something incredible.

The seven Mega Mantids began to *shrink*!

They went from mega to mini in a matter of seconds.

"How did *that* happen?" Lindsey asked. "I thought you said your dad's invention didn't shrink?"

"It didn't!" Ranger cried.

"Something must have happened when the RID mixed in with the shrinking formula that was left in the cans," I said.

Down on the ground, the Mini Mantids began to wriggle away.

"Hey!" Stella cried. "We can't let them go!"

Without thinking, I raised my foot and stomped. Hard. Bug guts splurted *everywhere*! It was like when Dad swatted the two flies at once in my room. With only a few strategically placed steps, I got every single mantis under my treads.

It was stomptacular!

But we weren't done with Mega Mantis yet.

We still had to search the entire Air Force Base to make sure we got all of the mantids. Then there was the problem of that headless mantis at the edge of the field. What were we supposed to do about that? Plus, we needed to find the original *Mega Mantis* reel and make sure no one had watched it and released *another* B-Monster into the world.

This was messier than my room at the end of the week.

Ranger and Stella were arguing about what

we should do first. They wanted to head back to Leery Castle to give Walter an update. But I nixed that idea.

I had a much better plan.

"Forget the castle," I said. "We need to get the reel and I have a feeling I know where it is. Walter can meet us there."

CHAPTER 15

THE DOCTOR IS IN

"Hurry! Hurry! Hurry!" I said. I liked being in charge. "We have to get to Dr. Von Rosenhof's place fast!"

I had a hunch that Dr. V's place was where all the trouble started. I'm no genius when it comes to vocabulary, but I get pretty good hunches.

Stella *hated* this hunch. She looked at me like Mega Mantis One looked at Mega Mantis Two before it chewed off its head.

We still had the spray cans on our backs when we climbed aboard our bikes. We'd used Stella's cell phone to call Walter. He said he would drive the limousine down to meet us right away.

As we pedaled along, I felt tired. I couldn't wait

to get my huge pack off my back. Everyone else's cans were drained from the mantis assault. I still had one full can of RID sloshing around inside mine.

Stella had been right about one thing. Dr. V's property was mysterious. We could hardly see the house from the road thanks to a giant fence. But I wasn't scared. What could be scarier than being attacked by giant mantids who escaped from a B-Monster movie?

We ditched our bikes and tiptoed behind a row of bushes toward an enormous bay window at the back. Inside was flickering blue. The four of us peered through the glass.

"We could just ring the front doorbell," Ranger said.

"Nah," Lindsey said, holding up her camera. "Sneaking is half the fun. Say parmesan, Jesse!"

He smirked. She snapped. Some guy was asleep on a chair inside, but the camera flash didn't make him move.

Off to the side of the guy's chair, I saw a television. I couldn't hear, but movie credits scrolled down the screen.

Directed by . . .

"Nooooooooo!" I wailed and banged on the glass.

"What are you doing?" Ranger said.

"You'll wake him up, dork!" Stella said, insulting me.

"I know!" I cried. "That's the idea. Look!"

The scrolling credits were from none other than *Mega Mantis*.

And Dr. V was watching the movie from a reel-to-reel projector!

"Let's go around to the front door!" I cried.

We rushed around the side of the house to ring the bell. As we moved past a row of bushes, I saw a dark figure lurking in the shadows by the front door. As we drew closer, it moved!

"Aaaaaah!"

"AAAAAAH!"

"Walter?"

"Monster Squad! There you are!" Walter cried. "I just parked the limousine. Shall we ring Dr. Von Rosenhof's bell?"

We nodded and I pressed the doorbell. It sounded more like a door gong.

All at once, a bright light flooded the front doorway and surrounding yard. Only then did I notice that Dr. V had enormous floodlights all over his yard. It was almost too bright to see.

Click, click, click.

I shivered as the door unlocked. What would Dr. V say to us, four random kids and Walter showing up at his creepy house out of nowhere? But even more importantly, how could we find out if his reel of *Mega Mantis* was an original reel?

"Hello?" Dr. Von Rosenhof said curiously as he opened the door. "May I help you?"

I was about to explain, when he saw Walter.

"Block! Walter Block! Is that you?"

Walter stepped right up and the two of them shook hands. They started to chat, but I wanted to get right to the point.

"Dr. Von Rosenhof," I said, interrupting, "are you watching the Oswald Leery movie *Mega Mantis* at this very moment?"

Ranger, Lindsey, and Stella looked impressed by my take-charge question, I could tell. But Dr. V looked at me funny.

"How on Earth did you know what I was watching?" Dr. V said.

"We saw from the window," Lindsey explained.

"And we know a little bit about that particular movie, sir."

"You were spying on me?" Dr. V asked.

"No!" we all cried at the same time. "We're not spies."

"So what *are* you?" he asked. "Walter? Are these kids with you?"

"We have a little bit of a situation on our hands, Von Rosenhof," Walter said quietly, as a form of explanation. "Can we come inside?"

Dr. Von Rosenhof pulled his front door wide open and the five of us pushed inside. Stella shoved in first, of course.

My eyes scanned the room. The inside of this house was how I imagined Dr. V's place might be, with insect parts on display. It was a little like Ranger's father's lab, but with more books and definitely more bugs. The lidded glass jars were everywhere! One entire shelf had different breeds of mantis—including a two-headed one.

But there was no time to look at jars now. I headed for Dr. V's projector and quickly removed the reel from the machine.

INSECTA MANITODEA

On the edge of the reel, I found an aging sticker with four little words I couldn't peel off: *Mega Mantis/Original Reel.*

"Oh no!" I blurted.

Stella rushed over. "Great," she groaned. "You found it."

"We need your help, Dr. Von Rosenhof," I said. "Oswald Leery needs your help. The human race needs your—"

"Get to the point," Stella snarled. "We think that the original *Mega Mantis* movie may be . . . mega *dangerous*."

"How many times have you watched this reel?" Lindsey added.

"Why do you keep asking me strange questions about the movie?" Dr. V replied.

"Because every time you watched this reel," Ranger explained, "a *real* Mega Mantis got loose."

"What?" Dr. V turned to Walter. "Is this true?"

"I'm afraid so," Walter admitted. "Leery had a few problems keeping the movie B-Monsters under control. They figured out a way into our world. It's a long story."

"According to my research, a mantis the size of Mega Mantis would—" Dr. Von Rosenhof gulped. "How many came through?"

"Eight," Stella said. "That includes seven we just zapped at the Air Force Base . . ."

"And one that lost its head at the Drive-O-Rama," Lindsey said.

"Although there may be more," Ranger piped up.

"More?" Dr. Von Rosenhof's face went white. "How many more?"

"It depends," I said. "How many times did you watch the original reel of *Mega Mantis*, Doctor?"

Dr. Von Rosenhof grabbed a pad of yellow

paper off a table and began to scribble. He was muttering to himself.

"Hmmm . . . let's see . . . I watched *Mega Mantis* once a few years back and then last month . . . and last week a few times . . ."

"How many in *all*?" Stella asked, as impatient as ever.

"I believe I watched the movie eight times in all," he said.

"Eight viewings. Eight dead bugs," Lindsey said. "Whew! So this is a wrap! That was such a close—"

"Not so fast!" I said, waving the reel in the air. "What about *tonight's* viewing, Dr. V?"

The doctor made a face like he'd just sucked a lemon.

"Oooh," Dr. Von Rosenhof said. "I'm afraid that I hadn't considered the most recent screening—"

I threw the reel on the ground and began to stomp on it. Stella joined in. Soon the four of us were stomping and kicking and shredding *Mega Mantis* into teeny bits. It was another stomptacular!

Dr. Von Rosenhof looked appalled. Walter, however, looked proud.

"Sorry for the mess," I said, bending down to pick up the pieces.

Bzzzzzzzzzzzt.

All at once, I felt a gnat on my neck. Then Stella, Ranger, and Lindsey saw a swarm of little bugs come into the room. We knew exactly what *that* meant.

Rrrrrrarrrrrrkkkkk!

Our eyes bugged out wide. We knew that noise. Boy, did we ever!

"Mega Mantis Nine!" we all yelled at the same exact time.

"Here?" Dr. Von Rosenhof asked. "At my house?"

"It must have been attracted to the really bright floodlights," I said.

"So what does the Monster Squad propose we do now?" Walter asked.

"Kiiiya!" Stella struck one of her karate poses.

"Oh no! We're all out of RID!" Lindsey said.

But then I remembered my backpack and the spray can that had malfunctioned. "We're not out of *anything*, Monster Squad," I said confidently. "We can zap this mantis just like the others."

Walter and Ranger grabbed my pack. Together

the bunch of us fiddled with the hose and lid. It took us a few minutes but we got it working properly again. Then we headed into Dr. V's front yard.

Mega Mantis Nine was right there, drooling.

"Stand back, everyone," I cried as I fixed up my spray. "Here, Mega Mega!"

There must have been sensors on Nine's knifelike pincers. He turned toward me with hunger in his freaky compound eyes. But I didn't waste a moment.

"Spray!"

At first the spray didn't come out very strong, but then it hit the bug with full force. It reeled and twisted and then, finally, it *shrunk*—just like the others.

We raced over. I leaned down and picked up the mantis by the legs. It was just like the time my dad picked up the flies, only *braver*. I handed Mini Mantis to Dr. Von Rosenhof.

"Insecta Manitodea!" Dr. V cried with glee. "This is the finest day of my scientific life. Thank you, Monster Squad."

He shoved the Mini Mantis into a small box from his pocket, and we said our good-byes.

Walter offered to give us all a ride home. We threw our packs into the trunk of his limousine so the smell of RID wouldn't fill up the backseat. When he popped the trunk, however, I noticed something strange. There was an open cooler back there with . . .

More jars.

"What are *these*?" I asked, lifting out one of the cold jars.

Were there bugs in here, too?

"AAAAAAAAAAAAAAAH!"

I nearly dropped one jar when I saw what was swimming inside.

Eyeballs?

"Look!" I cried, holding it up to the others.

Stella cringed. "I can't look at that when it's looking back at me!" she said.

"Don't mind the samples," Walter said coolly. "I'm doing a few experiments for Dr. Leery. I'll explain the next time you're at the castle."

Carefully, I put the jar back into the trunk. As curious as I usually am, I wasn't ready to talk about eyeballs or anything new right now. I was still reveling in our victory over nine Mega Mantis giants.

"Here's to teamwork!" I cried.

"What is that, Damon?" Lindsey asked.

"Yeah, Molloy, what *is* that?" Stella asked.

"Teamwork?" I groaned. "Duh! When people work together to do a positive thing . . ."

"No! No! What's *that*?" Ranger asked.

They were all pointing to my shirt. Of course, they were actually pointing to a small, black something *on* my T-shirt.

Another bug!

I glanced down. A week ago, the sight of even an itsy, bitsy, teeny, weeny bug like this would have sent me screaming to hide under Cowboy Pete, my beloved blanket.

But today, I'd faced the largest mantids known to man. I was a *real* cowboy. I squished that bug flat between my bare fingertips and growled, "Don't mess with the Mantis," in my best Roger Rogers accent.

Stella chuckled. "You mean, 'Don't mess with the Molloy,' don't you?"

"What a photo op!" Lindsey cried. She held up her camera. Stella and Ranger posed with me.

"Say cheese, everyone!" she said, just like a normal person.

I grinned. Of course it was just about the only normal thing about Lindsey, me, Stella, or Ranger right now.

But I was beginning to like it this way.

LOOK OUT FOR BOOK 3:
THE BEAST WITH 1000 EYES